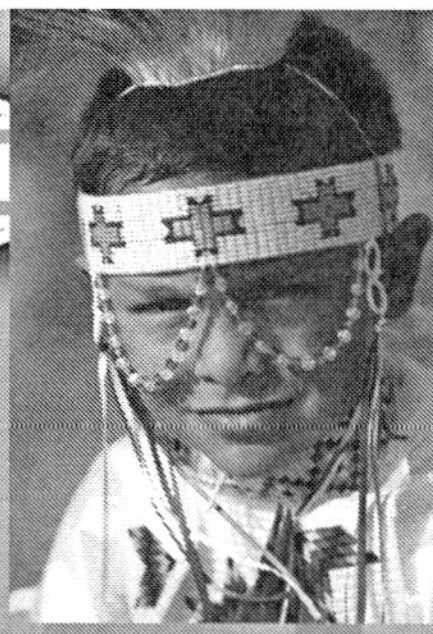   

Arizona Native Americans

A Kid's Look at ...
Chiefs, Tribes, ...
Powwows, Lore, and ...
The Past and the Present

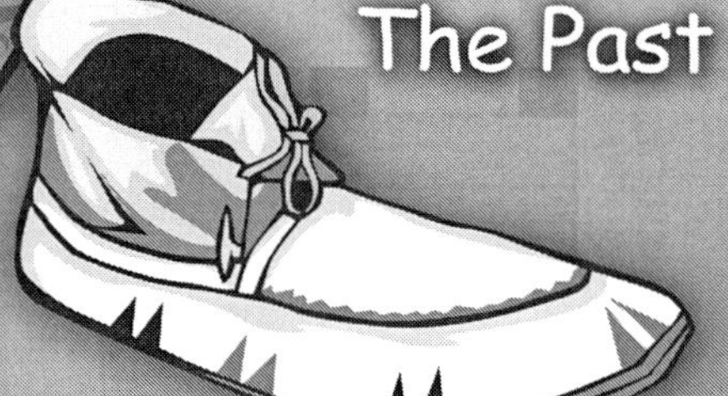

By Carole Marsh

Editors: Jenny Corsey and Teresa Valentine
Graphic Design: Lynette Rowe • Cover Design: Victoria DeJoy

Native American Heritage™

Carole Marsh Books

Published by
Gallopade International™
800-536-2GET
www.gallopade.com

Gallopade is proud to be a member of these educational organizations and associations:

The National School Supply and Equipment Association (NSSEA)
American Booksellers Association (ABA)
Virginia Educational Media Association (VEMA)
Association of Partners for Public Lands (APPL)
Museum Store Association (MSA)
National Association for Gifted Children (NAGC)
Publishers Marketing Association (PMA)
International Reading Association (IRA)
Association of African American Museums (AAAM)

Native American Heritage™ Series

Native American Big Activity Book

Native American Biographies

Native American Coloring Book

Native American Heritage Book

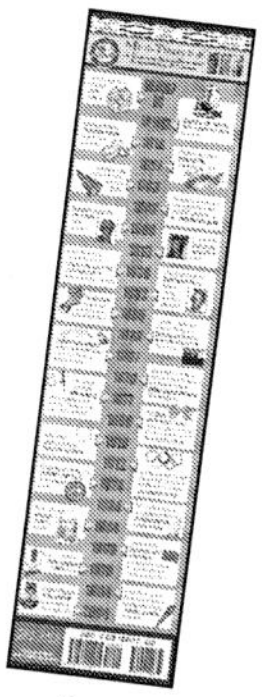

Native American Timeline

Arizona STATE STUFF™

- My First Pocket Guide: Arizona
- My First Book About Arizona
- Arizona Coloring Book
- The Big Arizona Reproducible Activity Book
- Jeopardy: Answers & Questions About Our State
- Arizona "Jography!": A Fun Run Through Our State
- Arizona Gamebooks
- Arizona Bingoes
- Arizona Illustrated Timelines
- Arizona Projects
- Arizona Bulletin Board Set
- Arizona PosterMap
- Arizona Stickers
- Let's Discover Arizona! (CD-ROM)

Word from the Author

Hello!

I hope you are as interested in North America's wonderful Indian heritage as I am!

Like most kids, I grew up thinking of Indians as the other half of Cowboys. Today, of course, we are getting a much clearer and more accurate picture of what the first peoples on our land were all about. These "facts" are much more fascinating than anything Hollywood can make up. And you probably won't find much of this information in your history textbook!

I am 1/16 Cherokee. This is something I am very proud of and happy about. My grandmother was 1/4 Cherokee. She had tan skin, long gray hair and a very Indian look – especially if I did something bad! Her maiden name was Carrie Corn. Of course, when she got married, she took her husband's name, so it was many years before I learned to appreciate the significance of my native heritage.

Today, I'm trying to make up for lost time by exploring my roots as deeply as I can. One of the most interesting things I've learned is how fascinating all of the Indian tribes are – in the past, the present and future!

As you read about "your" Indians, remember that all native peoples were part of an ever-changing network of time, ideas, power and luck — good and bad. This is certainly a history that is not "dead," but continues to change – often right outside our own back doors! – all the time.

Carole Marsh
She-Who-Writes

PS: Many references show different spellings for the same word. I have tried to select the most common spelling for the time period described. I would not want to be in an Indian spelling bee!

A is for . . .

Akimel O'odham

Also known as the Pima Indians. Their ancestral lands stretched from southern Arizona to northern Mexico. The Upper Pima (Pima Alto) lived along the Salt and Gila Rivers in Arizona. They were villagers, farmers, and did some hunting and fishing. Their pottery is polished red-and-black. Each village had a chief and was organized into two clans: the Red Ant clan and the White Ant clan, who opposed each other in games.

Awl

An Indian's "needle." Often made from wood, thorns, bone, or metal, it was used to punch holes in skins so they could be sewn together.

Altar

A platform made of rocks or animal skulls; some had bowls, feathers, rattles, or skins on them. Indians prayed at these altars for things like good crops or expert hunting skills.

Apache Wars

Series of major hostilities between the Apache, settlers, and U.S. troops that started in the 1860s and ran thru 1880s.

Arrowhead

The pointed tip of an arrow, made of bone, antler, wood, or iron. Some tips had barbs that would embed themselves in flesh. These barbs made it difficult for an enemy to remove the arrowhead from a wound.

Aborigine

A member of the earliest known population of a region.

Adze

An Indian woodworking tool used to cut, scrape, or gouge. Blades were made of stone, shell, bone or copper.

Apache

After getting the horse from the Spanish, they quickly became superior horsemen. Got their name from the Zuñi Indians; "apachu" means enemy. Primarily a nomadic tribe that roamed far and wide in the Southwest, they were best known for raiding before they were put on reservations. They are master coiled basket makers, with a complex mythology and well-defined society.

Atlatl

An atlatl is a device that looks like a wooden handle with a hook on the end, used to propel a spear-shaft. Atlatls were used widely by Indians in Arizona before the advent of the bow and arrow. The atlatl weight (a carved stone) was attached to the atlatl and is thought to have functioned as a counterbalance, allowing the spear to be delivered with greater accuracy and force.

Anasazi

The commonly used name for an Early Arizonan people who were ancestors of the Pueblo peoples. The Anasazi were descended from the early Basketmaker peoples of our area. They achieved great progress in the arts, architectural engineering and agriculture. They were ancestors of today's Pueblo Indians, and existed approximately from 100 B.C. to 1300 A.D. The modern Pueblo peoples object to the use of this term, which in Navajo means "enemy ancestors" and prefer Hisatsinom or Moqui.

B is for . . .

Band

A subdivision of an Indian tribe. In earlier times, a band was sometimes created when part of a tribe split off from the main group. The band also chose new leadership.

Betatakin

The word means "ledge house" in Navajo. Also the name of an ancient Anasazi pueblo in Tsegi Canyon at Navajo National Monument.

Buffalo

Once found in the area of the northern Chihuahan Desert. Hides were used for many things. Every tribe member was given a piece of the animal to eat. There were strict rules about not hunting buffalo alone, so that one person wouldn't scare them all away! To catch the animals, the hunters chased them off cliffs or encircled them in fire, then shot them.

Baskets

Some were woven and others were coiled. Baskets were made from roots, grasses, barks, and other natural materials. Northern Arizona Indians made coiled baskets with yucca and wicker baskets with wild currant and rabbit brush. Southern Arizona Indians used willow, squaw weed, skunk week, the root of the tule and devil's claw and yucca.

Bullroarer

Sacred instrument symbolizing rain, lightning and thunder. Made of a rectangular piece of wood and a cord. The wood is pine or fir and should come from trees that have been struck by lightning. A person would twirl the wooden part above the head, holding onto the cord, creating a distinctive sound.

Buckskin

Softened, smoke-treated rawhide. Used by some Arizona Indians to make clothes, bags and pouches.

Blankets

Used for door covers, partitions, bags, to dry food on, carry babies and many other purposes. Arizona Indians wove blankets from animal hair, skins, bark or feathers. The Navajo are known for their blankets.

Bow

Made from wood, horn or bone. Indian children learned how to use bows. The bowstring was made from animal gut, rawhide or twisted vegetable fibers.

Basketmaker Indians

Early Arizona peoples who lived in caves and underground dwellings called pit houses.

Big Mountain

Considered a place of healing to Navajo and Hopi. Center of the most recent land dispute (started in 1974) among the two tribes, federal government, and mining interests. Splits have happened in the tribes between traditionalists (who want to prevent the destruction of sacred lands) and tribal councils (who want the mining income). Oddly enough, the traditionalists of the two tribes are working together to prevent mining, even though the whole dispute started as a removal of Navajo from lands officially reserved for the Hopi.

Bone

Animal bones were used by Arizona Indians to make buttons, whistles and other items.

C is for . . .

Casa Grande

"Large House;" built by the Hohokam near Coolidge around A.D. 1350. This large 4-story building with a 35-foot stone tower is the oldest masonry construction project in the world.

Chief

Leader of a tribe. Different titles meant different things. Some members were made chief because they owned deeds to land. Chieftainship was often inherited, usually from the mother!

Code Talkers

Navajo who used their native language as coded combat communication during World War II (Marines, Pacific front) who were crucial to taking Iwo Jima.

Calendar Sticks

Sticks with carved markings to help the people remember their history over a number of years. Dots and circles were used for important ceremonies, and notches used to indicate things like earthquakes, waterworks building, Apache attacks, etc. The Papago (Tohono O'odham) are famous for these; they are passed down through the generations.

Canyon De Chelly

Site of Indian habitation; the Anasazi settled here around A.D. 700. Name means "rocky canyon. Located in northeastern Arizona.

Contact Period

What historians call the era in the 1500s when Native Americans first met Europeans. These meetings changed the lifestyle of the Arizona Indian more than anyone could ever have anticipated!

Clan

A tribal unit. Members are descended from the same ancestor.

Cochise

Chiricahua Apache chief who led the revolt of his tribe against the whites in the 1870s. After finally surrendering (undefeated in battle), he was very wise in peace, although the white man did not often listen to his ideas.

Cochise People

Archaic Period (6500-1500 B.C.) people of the Cochise Culture in southern and central Arizona. They were hunter-gatherers who evolved into farmers with the introduction of corn from cultures further south in present-day Mexico.

Coronado, Francisco Vásquez de

Spanish explorer who came to Arizona around 1540 hunting for fabulous cities of gold. After tormenting the local Indians for 2 years, yet finding nothing but the Grand Canyon, he left.

D is for . . .

Dance

There were Indian dances for every occasion: war, peace, hunting, rain, good harvests, etc. Drums, rattles, and flutes of bone or reed provided the music. Dancers often chanted or sang while performing. Steps were not easy to learn and required consistent practice.

Descendants

The first Arizona Indians were descendants of primitive hunters who crossed the Bering Strait from Asia to what is now Alaska. At that time, glacial ice still covered most of North America. These people were the true discoverers of the "New World!"

Desert Peoples

About 4000 B.C., nomadic hunters occupied the Grand Canyon region of Arizona. They made figures of sheep and antelope from split twigs. The desert people of southern Arizona hunted in roving bands and gathered seeds, berries and nuts.

Dyes

Made from natural materials by Indians in Arizona in the old days. Different colors were used depending on what materials were available and what objects were to be dyed. The Navajos combined rabbit brush and cedar ashes to obtain a yellow dye. Different parts of the sumac were used to create a variety of different dye colors. Yucca was also used to create black dye.

Dishes

Made from clay, bark, wood, stone, and other materials, depending on what was available and what food they would be used for.

Diné or Dineh

What the Navajo people call themselves.

Dreams

Important in the Indian tradition. It was believed that dreams were the "windows" to the soul. Many thought a person's hidden desires were expressed in dreams.

E is for . . .

Earring

Medicine men sometimes pierced male and female ears at special ceremonies. Earrings, which cost parents or relatives a significant amount, symbolized wealth and distinction. The more earrings that an Indian wore, the greater his honor. Some earrings measured 12 inches in length!

Effigy Jars

Those made by the Mojave were decorated with human-like features, and even with jewelry!

Everyone Should Visit

See these outstanding Arizona Indian places: Ak-Chin Indian Him-Dak Museum and Archives, The Amerind Foundation Archaeology Museum, Apache Culture Center and Museum, Arizona State Museum, Colorado River Indian Tribes Museum, Deer Valley Rock Art Center, Fort Apache, Gila County Historical Museum, Gila River Arts and Crafts Museum, The Heard Museum, Hopi Cultural Center, Hualapai Tribal Museum, Hubbell Trading Post, Mission San Xavier Del Bac, Mohave Museum, Montezuma Castle National Monument, Museum of Northern Arizona, Navajo Nation Museum. Navajo National Monument, Pueblo Grande Museum, Smoki Hall Museum, Tonto National Monument, Tusayan Ruin and Museum, Walnut Canyon, the Wupatki and Sunset Crater, Yavapai-Apache Visitor Activity Center.

Epidemics

Arizona Indians had no immunity to the diseases that white explorers, colonists and settlers brought to their lands. These diseases included smallpox, measles, tuberculosis and others, which ravaged the tribes in great epidemics that killed many, and sometimes all, members of a tribe.

Eagle

An animal used in many Indian ceremonies. Eagle feathers attached to war bonnets and shields communicated an Indian's rank in his tribe and what kinds of deeds he had done. Feathers also adorned rattles, pipes, baskets, and prayer sticks.

F is for . . .

First on the Land

Paleo Indians lived in Arizona as long ago as 10,000 B.C. Around Naco, archaeologists have unearthed tools and weapons of these early inhabitants who were expert hunters of prehistoric animals.

Fiddle

The Apache fiddle was an instrument whose soundbox was created from a yucca stalk. A single sinew string was attached to a tuning peg; it was played with a wood and sinew bow.

Fort Bowie

National historic site, stage station and fort at Apache Pass. For 30 years, center of military operations involved in the conflict between the U.S. military and the Chiricahua Apaches. Site of the Battle of Apache Pass, and where Geronimo surrendered in 1886.

Farmers

Many Arizona Indians, ancient and modern, have farming ways! Even pre-contact Indians tilled and irrigated, raising many important crops. Corn, cotton, beans, squash, melons, sunflowers, gourds, pumpkins and tobacco are all native Indian crops!

Famine

During a famine, the Tohono O'odham were known to move to the Akimel O'odham villages along the Gila River and work under the supervision of the host tribe to earn their keep!

Footwear

Arizona Indians wore different footwear depending on their tribe and environment. Moccasins were made mostly of animal skin. Sandals were made of rawhide or plant material.

Fetish

These small objects were thought to hold the spirit of an animal or a part of nature. A fetish could be an object found in nature, such as bone or wood, or it could be a carved object. The fetish was usually small enough to be carried in a small bag or on a cord. The making and use of a fetish was kept secret by its owner and only shared with the one who inherited it.

G is for . . .

Go To These Exciting Indian Events in Our State

All Indian Pow-Wow, Flagstaff; Annual O'odham Tash, Casa Grande; Arizona State University Spring Competition Pow Wow, Tempe; Canyon Echoes Pow Wow; Chinle; "Cowboy Days and Indian Nights" Contest Pow Wow, Page; Diné College Spring Contest Pow Wow, Tsaile; Flagstaff Indian Days, Flagstaff; Inter Tribal Contest Pow Wow, Hidden Springs; Navajo Nation Fair (the "World's Largest American Indian Fair"), Window Rock; New Year's Powwow, Tucson; Pueblo Grande Museum Auxiliary Indian Market, Phoenix; Scottsdale Indian Artists of America Show, Scottsdale; World Champion Hoop Dance Competition, Phoenix; and the Zuni Marketplace, Flagstaff.

Games

Adults played ball and other games of chance or skill. Indian children spun tops, fought pretend battles, did target-shooting, walked on stilts, played hide and seek, or competed to see who could hold their breath the longest!

Gans

Apache supernatural beings, the "Mountain Spirits" who brought agriculture to the people and are guardians of wildlife.

Gorgets

Beautiful ornaments hung around the neck or from ears; their significance, if any, is unknown.

Gourds

Hollowed-out shell of a gourd plant's dried fruit, which often grew into a specific shape. Indians raised many species of gourds. They were used for spoons, bowls, masks, rattles, and even storage.

Geronimo

Chief of the Chiricahua Apache. Refused to give in and live on a reservation for as long as possible. But in 1886, he surrendered and was sent first to a prison in Florida, then to Oklahoma where he died at the age of 80.

H is for . . .

Horses

Spaniards brought the horse to America. At first, Indians were afraid of the horse or thought it was sacred. Later, Indians "broke" horses gently, often "hypnotizing" them with a blanket. Horses were used for transportation, trade, barter or payment. Some Indians ate horse meat in hopes of gaining the animal's power.

Hisatsinom

The name the Hopi usually give to their ancient ancestors. Preferred by the Hopi to the Navajo word most commonly used: "Anasazi."

Hogan

The hogan is a residence and/or ceremonial dwelling for the Navajo. Originally built with a 5-sided forked-stick log frame. If extra insulation was needed, it might be entirely covered with packed adobe or mud, hiding the faceted shape. The door always faces east towards the rising sun. Six or eight sided hogans are a new style since the early 1900's. The arrival of the railroad brought large supplies of cross-ties, which could be laid horizontally to form walls of a larger, taller hogan. There are two styles of hogans: the male hogan and the female hogan.

Hopi

Name means "peaceful people." The Hopi ate very little meat because animals were so scarce. The Hopi grew corn, beans, and squash. The Hopi also planted cotton and are said to have tamed wild turkeys. Hopi women made beautiful baskets, clay bowls, and jewelry. The men hunted, farmed, and wove cloth for blankets, clothing and belts. These Indians still live on 3 fingerlike mesas called First, Second and Third.

Headman

Apache leader of a band, chosen for leadership abilities and military prowess.

Horn and Hooves

Indians used animal horn to make spoons and dishes. Hooves were made into rattles and bird beaks were used for decoration.

Hair

Indians used hair as a textile. Hair from bison, mountain sheep, elk, moose, deer, dog, rabbit, beaver, or even humans were used to weave cloth, make wigs, or stuff pillows, balls, dolls or drumsticks.

Hunters

Early Indian peoples were hunters who used wooden spears with stone points to kill many kinds of large mammals that are extinct today, such as mammoths and mastodons!

Hohokam

Early Indians (100 B.C. to 1500 A.D.) that lived first by the Salt and Gila Rivers, then in the Tucson Basin. They grew corn, beans, squash, tobacco and cotton irrigated by a complex network of canals. Food, medicines and construction materials came from desert plants. They traded with other Indians, wove cloth, made clay pottery and baskets. They even had sunken handball courts! The Hohokam may have done the first etching in the world at about 1000 A.D. on shells. Their name means "vanished ones" in the Pima language. It is believed that they are the ancestors of the Pima and Papago Indians.

Hatchet

A small, short-handled ax, primarily used as a tool, not as a weapon. When settlers moved in, stone hatchets were replaced with iron ones.

I is for . . .

Indian Tribes in Arizona

Include the Akimel O'odham (Pima), Apache, Chemehuevi, Cocopah, Havasupai, Hopi, Hualapai, Maricopa, Mojave, Navajo, Paiute, Quechan (Yuma), Tohono O'odham (Papago), Yaqui, and Yavapai.

Indian Ladder

Indians made ladders by trimming branches off a tree. Some were left at consistent intervals to provide steps.

Indian Revolts

When the Indians in Arizona got tired of the Spanish pushing them around, they began to revolt. In 1751, the Pima and Papago began to fight back. Then the Apache constantly raided and attacked missions and settlements. In 1781 the Yuma Indians battled the missions on their lands, killing many, but ultimately retaining control of their homeland for many more years. But after the Spanish, came the Americans and many more bloody conflicts with the U.S. military.

Indian Wars

In the 1860s, Arizona's Indian Wars broke out on a large scale. First, U.S. Army officer wrongly accused the Apache of kidnapping children and stealing cattle. The Indians then fought against former trader, scout, and Indian agent, Colonel "Kit" Carson. In 1868, the last treaty between the United States and an Indian tribe was signed. This made the Navajo homeland a reservation and survivors were allowed to return there. In 1869, the Hualapais surrendered. In 1872, the Chiricahua Apache were given their homeland as a reservation. The Yavapais surrendered to Indian fighter Gen. George Crook in 1873.

Indian

In 1493, Christopher Columbus called the native people he met in North America "Indians" because he mistakenly believed he had sailed to India! Today, this term includes the aborigines of North and South America.

Indian Summer

Common term for a period of mild weather that often surprises us in late autumn.

Indian Scout

This term, used to describe a guide, applied to Indians or Europeans.

J is for . . .

Just So You Know . . .

Today you can find many Arizona Indians that follow some traditional ways. But there are also many who are entrepreneurs, doctors, lawyers, educators and even politicians! Tribes in Arizona today make their living through farming, livestock ranching, mining, oil, gas and coal, forestry, gaming, tourism, arts and crafts, and even real estate enterprises! If you visit a reservation or cultural event, make sure you know visitor etiquette. Often dances are religious ceremonies and should be observed as such; religious dances should not be applauded. Photography, videotaping and drawing are all important issues – check with the tribe or individual before any is started. Find out more at www.arizonaguide.com/native American_1.asp

Jerked Meat

Thin strips of buffalo, elk, deer or other animal meat which is dried on racks in the sun; also called "jerky."

Jacal

A house built from adobe and wood.

Jesuits

Roman Catholic priests called Jesuits were among the first to meet and live with the North American Indians. Their writings, sent back to Europe, serve as one of today's best references to early Indian life. In 1687, a Jesuit missionary priest named Eusebio Francisco Kino began his ministry to the Pima and Papago Indians of Pimeria Alta, which extends into southern Arizona. Called the Padre on Horseback, he was a kind man who explored and established 26 missions, including San Jose de Tumacacori, built in 1696 north of Nogales, and San Xavier del Bac Mission, south of Tucson. In 1768, Francisco Tomás Garcés came to minister to the Indians, explored much of Arizona and helped establish two missions at Yuma.

Judicial Termination

Modern term to describe current efforts by various U.S. government agencies and officials (especially the judicial system) to legally decrease the sovereignty of independent Indian tribes.

K is for . . .

Killed Pottery

Pottery placed in a grave as an offering to the dead person was called killed pottery. A hole was formed in its base during creation. Often broken pottery was placed in a grave because Indians believed the spirit of the dead person would then be released and could travel.

Kayenta

Regional group of the Anasazi that were in northeast Arizona. Excellent potters. The Navajo National Monument in Arizona preserves a principal home of these prehistoric peoples.

Kiva

Sunken ceremonial chamber. The religious and ceremonial life of the Hopi centers in the kiva, which is wholly or partly subterranean and entered by way of ladder through an opening in the flat roof.

Kuibit

A long pole made from the ribs of a saguaro cactus, used to knock down the cactus fruit. The fruit of the saguaro cactus is a delicacy – Indians to this day eat it fresh, boil it into jam or syrup (this syrup is also made into wine), or dry it for eating or grinding into powder to mix with water for a drink!

Keet Seel

One of the best-preserved cliff dwellings in Arizona; has 160 rooms and 6 kivas. Located in the Navajo National Monument. Name means "broken pottery."

Kokopelli

A mythological hump-backed flute player in most Southwestern Pueblo cultures that is well-known, even to non-natives. This spiritual figure represents many things, such as fertility and rain. Also known as Kokopilau, Kokopeltiyo and Kokopele.

Kachinas

Hopi spirits or gods which lived within the mountains. Hopi dancers would dress like Kachinas to represent, or stand for, the gods. Wooden Kachina dolls were made to teach the children about the gods. The Hopi believed the Kachina costume gave magic power to the man who wore it. They felt a man needed magic to talk to the gods. Hopi Kachinas talked to the gods by singing and dancing.

Knife

Made from various materials such as bone, reed, stone, wood, antler, shell, metal, or animal teeth (bear, beaver, etc.), knives were used as weapons but also creative handiwork.

L is for . . .

Lost Tribes of Israel

This historic theory has been floating around since 721 BC. The 10 lost tribes of Israel are supposedly groups of people gathered together by Sargon, the King of Assyria. Some say he cast out 10 of the 12 tribes of Israel. Many have tried to prove that the American Indians are these missing tribes!

Lance

Spear used for hunting and war. The hunting lance had a short shaft and a broad, heavy head. The war lance was light and had a long shaft.

Linguistic Families

There are 56 related groups of American Indian languages. A few of these speech families include Iroquoian, Algonquian, Siouan, Muskogean, Athapascan, and Wakashan.

Leggings

Both men and women wore cloth or skin covering, which were often decorated with quills, beads, or painted designs, for their legs.

Long Walk

The tragic winter 1864 march of the Navajo Indians and some Apache forced by "Kit" Carson. 8,000 Indians were forced to give up their homelands and relocate to a "reservation" in the eastern part of New Mexico that was more like a prison camp. About 200 men, women and children died along the 300-mile trail because of the bitter cold and lack of food. At Bosque Redondo, labor was forced, land was unfarmable, water was bad, food and fuel were very scarce, and disease was running rampant. During the four years there, 25% of the people died!

Lariat

These throw ropes made of rawhide, buffalo hair, or horsehair sometimes measured up to 20 feet long!

M is for . . .

Maize

Also called Indian Corn. Known as a "cereal" plant because it probably began as some form of grass. The Indians in our state figured out every possible way to use corn as a food. The only thing the white man added was the creation of "corn flakes!"

Medicine

Medicine could be good or bad. Medicines or charms were placed in a bag by young warriors and carried at all times. Some of the roots, leaves and bark that Indians in our state used as medicine are being rediscovered and used by today's doctors!

Massacre Cave

Site in Canyon de Chelly where more than 115 Navajo died in a battle with the Spanish military in 1805. There are conflicting accounts of what happened; the official military record indicated casualties of 25 women and 90 warriors, while another version claims those who were taking shelter in the cave were children, women and the elderly.

Metate and Mano

The Anasazi mortar and pestle used to grind corn.

Mogollon

Lived in the mountains and forests of that are close to the southern and eastern Arizona borders. They were probably descendants of the Cochise People, living from about 300 B.C. to 1300 A.D. These prehistoric peoples hunted game, gathered nuts and berries and cultivated crops. They traded with the Anasazi and are considered the first Southwest Indians to have built houses, made pottery, and farmed. Late in their era, about 900 A.D., the subgroup called the Mimbres culture produced their famous black-on-white style of pottery.

Masks

A face covering made from wood, basketwork, pottery or hides. Arizona Indians carved, painted and decorated masks with shells, fiber, hair, or feathers. Each mask had a special meaning.

Montezuma Castle

A 5-story high, 20 room Sinagua Indian cliff dwelling in the Verde Valley. Over 600 years old and one of the best preserved.

Missions

Religious centers where the missionaries worked trying to convert Indians. Most included a church, and many included farms or other industries overseen by the missionaries where natives often worked.

Mojave

The Mojave desert is named for the Mojave tribe. They built two different dwellings - one for warm weather, another for cold weather. They did hunt, fish and gather some, but they were primarily farmers. They traveled from the area around the present-day borders of Arizona, California and Nevada to the Gulf of California on trading trips. The Mojave were known as fierce fighters. War parties had 3 groups - archers, clubbers and stickmen.

Moqui

A Hopi word which means "the dead"; for them referring to their ancestors. A preferred term to "Anasazi".

N is for . . .

Native Americans

There are 17 major tribal groups in Arizona. The Navajos are the largest in number. About 5% of Arizonans are Native American, the 3rd most after California and Oklahoma. Arizona has about 252,000 Indian residents. Most live on the state's 20 reservations, which cover about 27% of the land area or 20 million acres!

Niman Kachina

A 16-day Hopi summer festival. The Snake Dance (a rain dance) is performed last. Kachinas danced with live snakes wrapped around necks and arms, even in their mouths. The snakes were later released outside the pueblo.

Needle

The kind of needle we think of for sewing was very rare among the Arizona Indians. They did have some needles made from bone, wood, cactus spines and other natural materials. The metal needle was brought with settlers. Thread used included horsehair, human hair and plant fibers.

Navajo National Monument

Here you can see three of the most-intact cliff dwellings of the ancestral Puebloan people (Anasazi). The monument is on the Shonto Plateau, which overlooks the Tsegi Canyon system in the Navajo Nation in Northern Arizona.

Names

Indian names were often changed during one's lifetime. These names could be derived from events that happened during the person's birth, childhood, adolescence, war service, or retirement from active tribal life. Some names came from dreams, some were inherited, and sometimes names were stolen or taken in revenge. Today some Indians maintain old, traditional Indian names, while others take modern names. Since settlers often did not read or write Indian languages, they recorded Indian names phonetically (as they "sounded"). Thus Indian names were often misspelled.

Navajo

One of America's largest Native American groups with over 250,000 people. Once they lived a nomadic life, frequently raiding other tribes. Their success as a tribe can be attributed to the way they adapted themselves over time by learning new skills and utilizing technology from other tribes. After the arrival of the Spanish and the horse, they raised large livestock herds, made huge advances in arts and crafts, and became master horsemen. The Navajo have the largest Indian reservation in the U.S. - 18,433,920 million acres. Most of it is in Arizona, with some in New Mexico and Utah. They are world-famous for their woven blankets and rugs, baskets, silver work, and sandpainting. More than 97% of Navajo adults still speak their language today!

O is for . . .

Oraibi

Hopi village built on the Third Mesa around the year 1100; the oldest settlement in the United States that has been lived in continuously. The site has moved over time, though; the present-day village is above the original site at the base of the mesa.

Over The Top

After the autumn harvest, the Havasupai moved – they climbed the walls of Cataract Canyon to the top of the plateau and lived in temporary camps among game for the winter!

Oral Chants

This Navajo art form is used in healing ceremonies. They are especially long recited legends and myths with musical accompaniment. There are a large number of episodes to each chant and hundreds of songs!

Oddly Enough

Turkeys were kept by the Hopi in tamed flocks, which helped provide meat and feathers!

Orators

Many Indian leaders were excellent public speakers. Powerful and dramatic speakers were vital to leaders who wanted to influence their tribe. Watch for famous Indian quotations in literature and textbooks! One example is Cochise. This is what he said:

"I do not think you will keep the peace. Once again you tell me we can stay in our mountains and our valleys. That is all we wish, we do not want to fight and kill whites, and we do not want the whites to fight and kill us. We want nothing but to live in peace. But I do not believe you will allow us to remain on the lands we love. I warn you, if you try to move us again, war will start once more; it will be a war without end, a war in which every Apache will fight until he is dead. Prove to me that I am wrong; prove to me that this time I can trust you."

P is for . . .

Pueblo Indians

When the Spanish first came to the Southwest, they found that Indians living in towns, while others were nomadic. The village-dwellers were called pueblos, the Spanish word for towns. Pueblos were not a single tribe, but several groups who shared a common culture. The Pueblo people of the Southwest have lived in the same location longer than any other culture in the United States!

Powwow

The original form of the word meant "medicine man." Medicine men would often use noise motion and confusion to scare away harmful spirits and cure people. It was also a gathering to talk about political matters. Today, the powwow is an event where Indians gather to sing, perform ceremonial dances, and share cultural pride and traditions.

Patayan

Early peoples in the Colorado River Valley of western Arizona and the Prescott area. May have been ancestors of the Yuma Indians.

Prehistoric Cultures

Arizona's 3 great prehistoric cultures were the Anasazi on the northern plateau, the Hohokam in the south-central desert and the Mogollon in the east-central mountains. Other groups included the Salado, Patayan and Sinagua people.

Pueblo Grande Museum

Located in Phoenix, at some village ruins of the Hohokam civilization.

Prayer Sticks

Used by the Havasupai in religious ceremonies. Also used by the Apache, Navajo and other Pueblo Indians. Usually they are wood, often painted, carved and adorned with turkey feathers.

Pottery

Indian pottery was made from built-up spirals of clay that were molded or paddled, or a combination of the two methods. Most pottery served as cooking vessels.

Picture History

Some Indians kept a record of time and important events by painting or drawing pictures or symbols on skin, bark, or stone.

Papoose

An American Indian infant aged between birth and one year is called a papoose. A papoose spent most of his or her days snugly wrapped in a kind of cradle made of skins or bark and a wooden frame that hung on the mother's back. This sturdy frame also allowed a mother to lean her papoose against a tree or rock within sight as she worked.

Paint

Indians used many natural materials to make paint, like clay mixed with oil or grease. Yellow "paint" was made with the gall bladder of a buffalo! Indians used paint to look scary or beautiful, to disguise themselves, or to protect their skin from sunburn or insect bites. Indians often applied red paint because it symbolized strength and success. That is why settlers often referred to the Indians as Red Men.

Pueblo

Name for the type of dwelling the Hopi live in. They are rectangular in shape, made of stone and mud, and often are several stories. Upper stories are reached by ladders. Timbers can be seen at the top of the walls to support the roof.

Q is for . . .

Quiver

Case used to hold arrows; made of woven plant materials or animal skins.

Quechan Indians

Also known as the Yuma Indians, in particular the tribal name of the Fort Yuma Indians. They are from the Arizona/California border area, centered around Yuma. Their environment was very hot and arid, and they were noted by Spanish explorers as nearly naked in dress, wearing only rawhide sandals, the occasional breechcloth (men) and bark aprons (women). They were farmers and often warlike, tall and powerfully built. They drove off the Spanish missionaries only one year after the two area missions were founded. From that time on, the Quechan retained control of their lands completely until the 1880s, unlike many other Southwestern tribes. Today they can be found on the Fort Yuma and Cocopah Reservations in Arizona.

Quirt

A short riding whip with a wood, bone, or horn handle.

Quillwork

Indians used the quills of porcupine or birds to make a type of embroidery. Quills were dyed with juice from berries and other materials. When they were ready to be used, the quills were either mashed with teeth or softened with hot water and flattened with rocks. The quills were then laced into moccasins, shirts, pipe covers, and other items. Beads which Indians received by trading with settlers eventually replaced quillwork.

Quotation

"There is no climate or soil which, to my mind, is equal to that of Arizona. We could have plenty of good cultivating land, plenty of grass, plenty of timber and plenty of minerals in that land which the Almighty created for the Apaches. It is my land, my home, my fathers' land, to which I now ask to be allowed to return. I want to spend my last days there, and be buried among those mountains. If this could be I might die in peace, feeling that my people, placed in their native homes, would increase in numbers, rather than diminish as at present, and that our name would not become extinct."

Geronimo, asking for the return of his Apache band to their native lands, 1905

R is for . . .

Rain Dancing

The rain dance ceremony, performed to encourage rainfall, was common among Indian religions because good weather is vital for a successful harvest. Rainmakers were in tune with nature; there are actual reported cases of Indians producing or preventing rain!

Roots

Indians used plant roots for food, medicine, dye, baskets, cloth, rope, salt, flavoring, and just to chew!

Rattles

Indians of Arizona made rattles from bird beaks, animal hooves, bones, pods, seashells, turtle shells and other animal parts. The rattles are used in ceremonies.

Rugs

Both the Navajo and Hopi are famous for their woven rugs featuring bright colors and geometric designs.

Rawhide

Untanned animal hide. The "green" hide was stretched on the ground or over a frame. Flesh and fat were removed. The skin was dried, washed, then buried with wood ashes which made the hair come off. Used by the Arizona Indian to make sandals, drumheads, and lashing; also used to mend broken objects and in many other ways.

Reservations

The U.S. government set aside, or "reserved," land for the Indians. These reservations originally served as a sort of prison during the beginning stages of Indian removal. At that time, reservations provided the government with some control over Indian activity and residency. This land was usually considerably less desirable land than the Indians' native territories. Today's reservations are lands that are tribally held, yet protected by the government. And the people are free.

S is for . . .

Salado

Early peoples who occupied cliff dwellings along the Salt River in Arizona. They left behind petroglyphs in the Eagletail Mountains and thought to have lived from 800 A.D. to 1450 A.D.

Shaman

Medicine man and spiritual leader who was supposed to have special healing power from another world.

Sipapu

The Hopi word for the navel of the Earth from which distant Puebloan ancestors are said to have emerged as they entered the present world. This word also can mean the small hole or indentation in the floor of a kiva which symbolizes the people's Earthly origin.

Sign Language

A way for Indians to communicate with others from a tribe whose language they did not speak.

Sweatlodge

Structure used for ritual purification by sweating from exposure to very hot fires or hot steam from pouring water over hot stones. Also called a sweathouse, for some tribes also doubling as clubhouses.

Shield

A piece of "armor" made of a rawhide-covered frame, which was carried into battle. Shields also could be decorative and religious objects. Many tribes make shields today as an art form!

Sinagua

Early Arizona peoples who farmed in the Flagstaff and Verde Valley areas. They lived in cliff dwelling and pueblos between 500 A.D. to 1300 A.D.

Sandpainting

The Navajo probably adopted this from other Southwest Indians. Sandpaintings are sacred art, used in healing ceremonies. The traditional principal colors are white, yellow, blue and black. The colors come from powdered minerals, crushed charcoal and sand. Sandpaintings are made by trickling the powders in patterns on clean sand to form a large picture. This is done by the medicine man and destroyed at the end of the ceremony. The Navajo make smaller sandpaintings today to sell, but they are very different in color, content and style from the sacred sandpainting!

Signals

Indian signs made with a pony, blanket, mirror, smoke, fire-arrow or other item to communicate over long distances.

Saddle

While some Indians did use saddles on their horses, most rode bareback!

T is for . . .

Tobacco
A sacred plant early Indians used to make offering to their gods, cure diseases, bring good luck, seal agreements and bind treaties.

Treaties
Written agreements between the U.S. government and the Indians, most of which involved the Indians giving up their native lands.

Tattoo
There were many Indians that tattooed themselves! In the Southwest, both men and women had tattoos on their faces, limbs and/or torsos. Common among the Mojave in Arizona.

Tuzigoot National Monument
A 110-room Sinagua pueblo. The oldest sections were build around 1000 A.D.

Tonto National Monument
Near Roosevelt Lake; site of the ruins of the ancient Salado peoples in Arizona.

Tomahawk
A club, axe or hammer used to chop wood, drive stakes in the ground or as a weapon.

Tracking
To follow a trail by finding a sign such as a broken blade of grass, a moved stone or moccasin track. Indians learned to trail as children, so that they could find food, track enemies and disguise their own signs.

Tusayan Ruin
Anasazi site in the Grand Canyon that dates back to 1185.

Tribe
A group of Indians with shared culture, history, original territory, ancestry, social organization, and governmental structure. A tribe may contain several bands of Indians.

Tohono O'odham
Also known as the Papago Indians. Their ancestral territory was in the Sonoran Desert. They were semi-nomadic and moved between two village locations known as "field villages" and "well villages". At one village they farmed, and at the other (near mountain springs) they hunted. Villages were divided into the Buzzard and Coyote clans. The Tohono O'odham have four reservations in Arizona, at Maricopa, Gila Bend, San Xavier, and Sells. Papago to this day make their beautiful, famous coiled baskets.

Thunderbird
A mythological Indian figure, as well as a part of the constellations for many Indians. Thunderbird mythology is mostly different from tribe to tribe, in general either coexisting with ancestors as an actual bird, or appearing as a spiritual nature god. The Thunderbird was good to the people in either case. Much mythology ties the thunderbird with thunder, lightning and storms.

U is for . . .

U.S. Bureau of Indian Affairs

Provides public services such as law enforcement, land records, economic development, and education to Indians. Known for mismanagement and ethical problems.

U.S. Indian Reorganization Act

Passed by Congress in 1934, the act authorized Indian tribes to establish and conduct their own governments, and to form businesses.

U.S. Indian Schools

The Bureau of Indian Affairs operates hundreds of federal schools around the nation. Enrollment of Native American children measures in the thousands!

Universities and Colleges

Study Native Americans at Arizona State University, University of Arizona, Diné College, and Tohono O'odham Community College!

U.S. Colonists

Called Long Knives or Big Knives by early Indians, who also called English explorers "Coat Men."

U.S. Indian Wars

The U.S. War Department has compiled an official list of "Indian Wars" that occurred in the United States. Over 50 wars were fought between the U.S. and the Indians during the period of 1790-1850.

U.S. President

Once called Great White Father by Indians.

V is for . . .

Viikita

Akimel O'odham (Pima) and Tohono O'odham (Papago) harvest celebration every 4th year, with costumed and masked dancers and clowns.

Victorio

Apache chief, leader of the Warm Springs band, forced to relocate with the band to the San Carlos Reservation in Arizona. He was best known as a master raid and battle planner, eluding all his pursuers. The conflict sometimes referred to as the Victorio War in 1879 was a series of battles centered around his band's attempt to return to Warm Springs.

Very Hungry

The Paiute, who here hunters, gatherers and foragers, often ate whatever they could find! How hungry would you have to be to eat what they sometimes ate: lizards, grubs and insects?

Volcanic Soil

When Sunset Crater began erupting around A.D. 1064, rich volcanic ash fell to the ground, which enriched the soil for farming. This caused Indian groups to migrate to such parts of the state, and started a period of amazing cultural, social and technological advancement with the different groups of these prehistoric people.

Villages

Many Arizona Indians lived in villages! Villages were formed around different clans or bands within the tribe, but could also contain different clans living together. Villages were usually permanent settlements, although semi-nomadic tribes have been known to migrate between permanent villages.

W is for . . .

War Dance

Indian braves danced this before going into battle. The dance was a way of assembling the braves and getting them to commit to the fight ahead.

Window Rock

Navajo tribal headquarters; named for a natural arch almost 50 feet wide.

White Man

Indians generally called them Pale Face, a name the white men themselves suggested!

War Club

A weapon made of stone, bone, or wood in the shape of a club.

Weaving

The Arizona Indians are famous in history and today for their weaving! The ancestral people wove their own cotton cloth, and their skills became more refined over time, passed on to the tribes we know today. The Navajo are world famous weavers, specializing in rugs and blankets in geometric designs and bold colors.

War Pony

Horse, often painted with colorful paint and ridden into battle.

Walnut Canyon

Site of a number of cliff dwellings of the Sinagua prehistoric peoples who lived here from about 1100 A.D. to 1250 A.D.

Wupatki

Sinagua and other ancestral ruins of hundreds of multistory homes north of Flagstaff. There are over least 2,668 prehistoric sites at this national monument!

Wickiup

A type of Indian dwelling that is domed or conical and made of a pole frame covered with a natural material or animal skins. The Apache lived in wickiups.

XYZ are for . . .

Yuma Territorial Prison State Park

Built in 1876 on the banks of the Colorado River in the middle of the desert. Local Yuma Indians were paid $50 a head to catch escapees!

Yucca

A member of the agave family with stiff green sword-like leaves (with sharp needled ends) and white flowers on a tall stalk. The plant had many uses: medicinal, ceremonial, arts and crafts, games, food, and dye. The yucca was also used as a material for weaving; Arizona Papago weavers still use this material today.

Yaqui

American Yaqui are descendants of the Mexican Yaqui who fled over the border to Arizona during the period of forced labor by the Mexican government that began in the 1880s. Today there are six Yaqui communities in AZ, located in Eloy, Marana, Pascua, Scottsdale, Tempe and Tucson.

Yavapai

Sometimes this tribe was referred to as Mojave Apache or Yuma Apache. Their ancestral lands were in western Arizona. The tribe had three major divisions. Nomadic farmers, hunters and gatherers, they were very independent, resisted missionaries, and fought settlement. One well-known member of this tribe was Carlos Montezuma. Although taken from the tribe as a child, in the late 1800s and early 1900s he was active in Indian affairs, agencies and schools across the nation, authored 3 books and founded the Indian magazine Wassaja in 1916.

Yush

Apache supernatural being, the "Giver of Life" who is the most powerful of all the beings.

Y... Or, "Why?"

1. Why do you think Indian warriors carried charms with them? Some Indian medicines have been scientifically proven to have true healing power and are still used today. Do you think their charms had any real power to help them win battles?
2. Why do you think the American government kept relocating Indians onto reservations and then making the reservations smaller and smaller?
3. Why did Indians use items such as a pipe in ceremonies? What kinds of symbolic objects do we use in ceremonies today?
4. Why and how did Indians use natural materials in creative ways?
5. Many Indian tribes are running successful businesses on their reservations today. There is one industry that many tribes are making a lot of money at. Do you know what this is? Hint: "I'll bet you do!"

Which Famous Native American Am I?

Solve the puzzle!

Word Bank

Black Elk	Crazy Horse	Sitting Bull	Sequoia
Sacajawea	Chief Joseph	Geronimo	Pocahontas

Down

1. This Shoshone woman joined Lewis and Clark as their guide and translator and helped make the expedition a success! Hint: She has 4 "a"s in her name!
4. This man gave the Cherokee their first alphabet so that they could write. Until then, they communicated only by speaking and drawing pictures. Hint: A famous ancient tree also has the same name!
5. He was one of the fiercest of Indian warriors! He fought against white settlers in Arizona and New Mexico to keep his people from being pushed off their lands. Hint: Jump!

Across

2. A legend says that this brave Algonquian woman saved the life of Englishman John Smith. Hint: Disney produced a movie about her.
3. He fought at Little Bighorn when he was only 13! He was also a wise "shaman" who saw visions and could advise people. Hint: Part of his name is an animal with antlers!
6. He was a great Sioux warrior who won the battle against General Custer at Little Bighorn in 1876. Hint: His horse was not crazy!
7. A leader of the Lakota (Sioux) tribe who lived on the Standing Rock Reservation in North Dakota after the battle of Little Bighorn. He tried to make conditions better for his people there, so the U.S. government called him a "troublemaker." Hint: He did not sit all the time!
8. A wise and brave chief of the Nez Percé who tried to bring his people to Canada to escape war. He said, "From where the sun now stands, I will fight no more forever." Hint: His father's name was "Old Joseph."

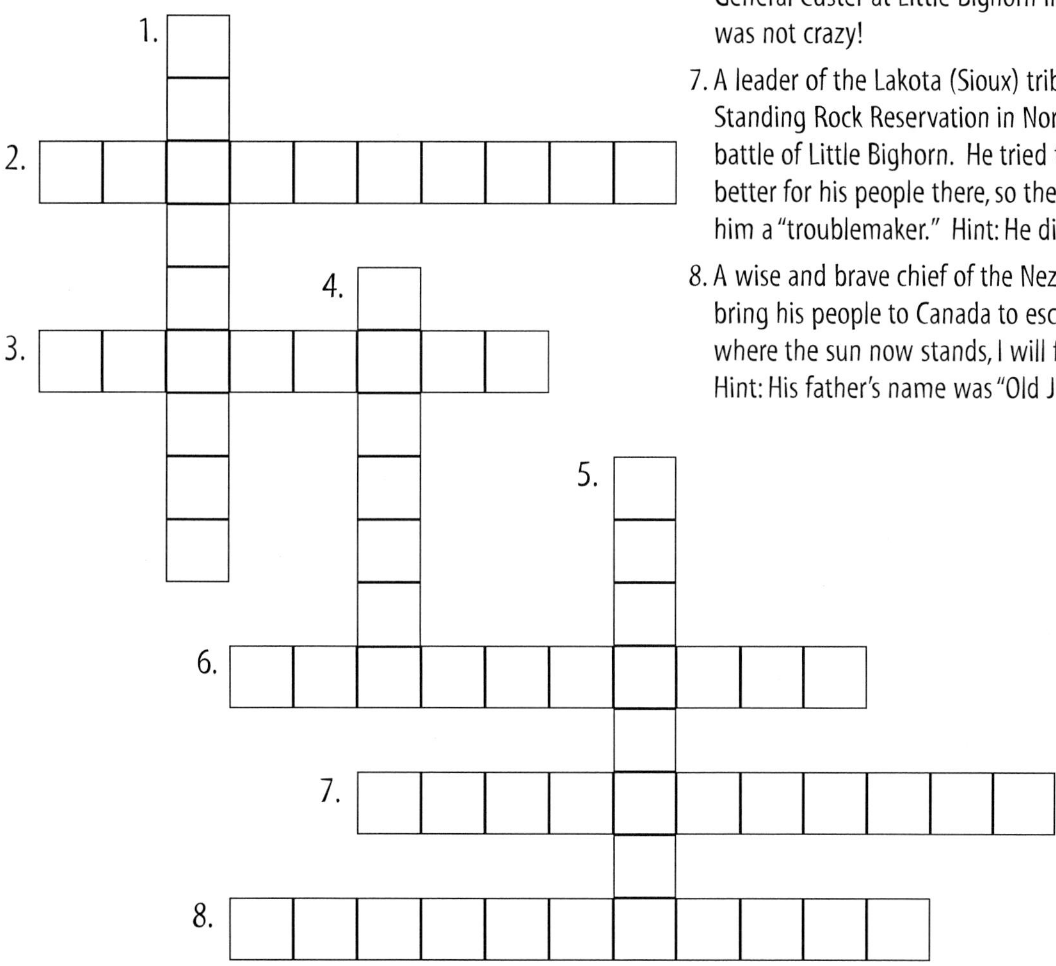

Answer Key: 1. Sacajawea; 2. Pocahontas; 3. Black Elk; 4. Sequoia; 5. Geronimo; 6. Crazy Horse; 7. Sitting Bull; 8. Chief Joseph

Different Ways for Different Indians!

North American Indian tribes are divided into different areas. In each of these areas, tribes shared common ways of living with each other. They might make similar arts or crafts, they might eat the same foods, or they might have had the same beliefs. These activities are all part of their "culture." Each area had its own culture, which was different from the tribes in all the other areas.

Below is a map of all the different groups of Indian tribes in North America. Color each area with a different color. You will see a colorful picture of how Native Americans can all be called "Indians" but still have very different cultures!

Celebration!

Powwows are big festivals where Native Americans gather to sing, dance, and eat together. It is a time to celebrate and show pride in their culture. Powwows can last from one afternoon to several days. The Indians dress in native costumes and dance ancient dances to the beating of drums.

Artists sell their arts and crafts. You might be able to buy some real Native American food cooked on an open fire. Native Americans go to powwows to be with each other, share ideas, and just have fun! Most powwows are also open to people who are not Indian. It's a great place to learn about Native American culture!

If you went to a powwow this weekend, what do you think you would see? What do you think might NOT be there? Circle the objects you think you would see at a powwow. Put an X through those you probably won't see.

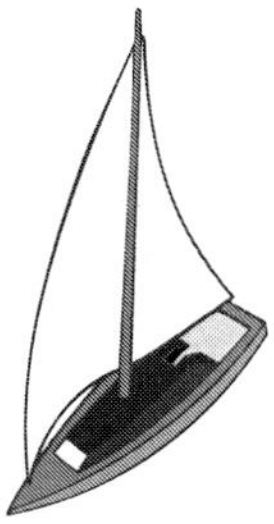

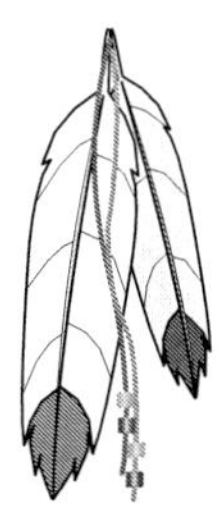

Answer Key: Circled objects are: beads, moccasins, open fire, drums, feathers, baskets, kids, food, drums, horse.

Make an Indian Weaving!

Many Native Americans used weaving to create useful things like sashes (belts), bags, mats, and blankets. They used animal hair to make yarn, and dyed the yarn with natural dyes from fruits and other plants. They also used some plant fibers, like cotton, to make weaving thread.

Weave a small Native American mat of your own. Use different colors of yarn to create a beautiful pattern in your weaving. Place a favorite object on the mat or hang it on your wall!

Prepare the "loom"

Cut a piece of cardboard 5 inches wide and 6 inches long. Along the two 5-inch sides (the "short" sides), have an adult cut slits 1/4 inch deep. These slits should be 1/2 inch apart from each other. So, on each short side you will have 9 slits.

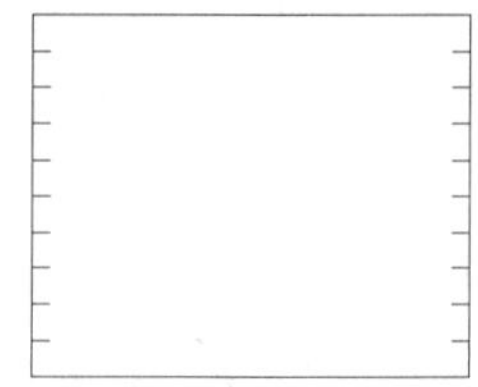

Directions:

1. Take a long piece of yarn and bring it from the back through the first slit (the one next to the edge of the cardboard.) The end of the yarn will hang down behind the cardboard.

2. Bring the yarn right across the front of the cardboard to the slit opposite the one your yarn came through.

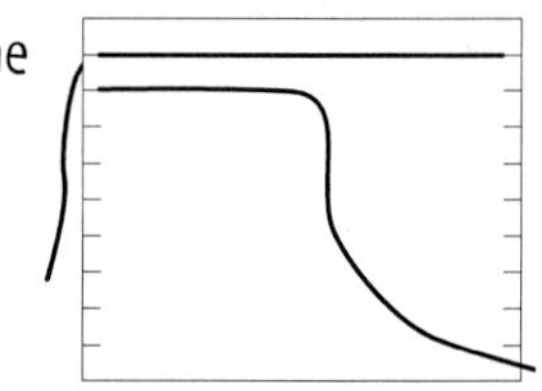

3. Now bring the yarn under the back of the cardboard and then up again through the second slit.

4. Repeat #2 and #3, until you have 9 strands of yarn across the front of your cardboard!

5. Then cut the yarn and tie the two loose ends in the back of the cardboard.

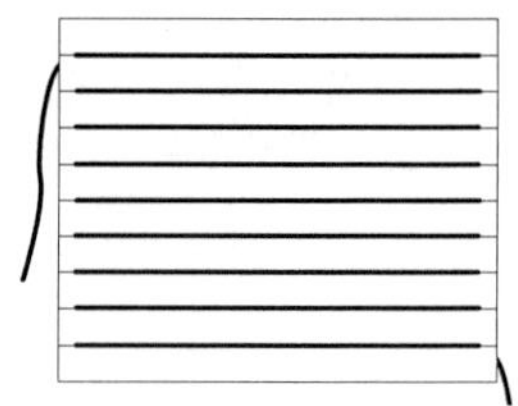

6. Take another piece of yarn and start feeding it through the 9 strands, going over one, under the next over the next, etc. When you get to the end, pull the yarn behind the cardboard and around to the front, and begin again. This time, whatever strand you went over, go under. And whatever strand you went under, go over.

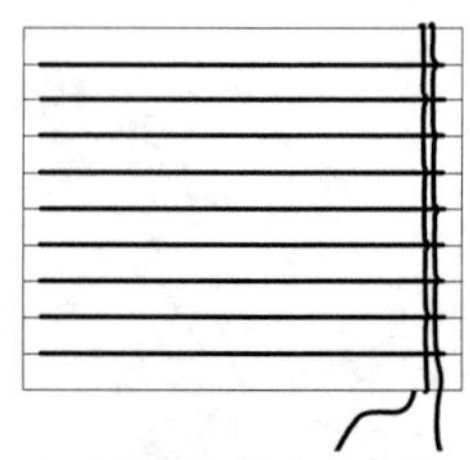

7. Repeat this pattern until the front of your cardboard in covered. Then cut the yarn in the back of the cardboard, and trim it to create a fringe for your mat!

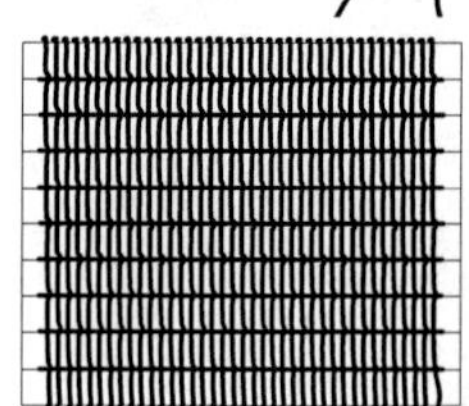

Tips:

- For a wild look, use variegated or different colored yarn!
- For a tighter mat, push the under/over strands up against the previous strands during weaving.
- To keep your mat from unravelling, tie neighboring fringe together up close to the mat.

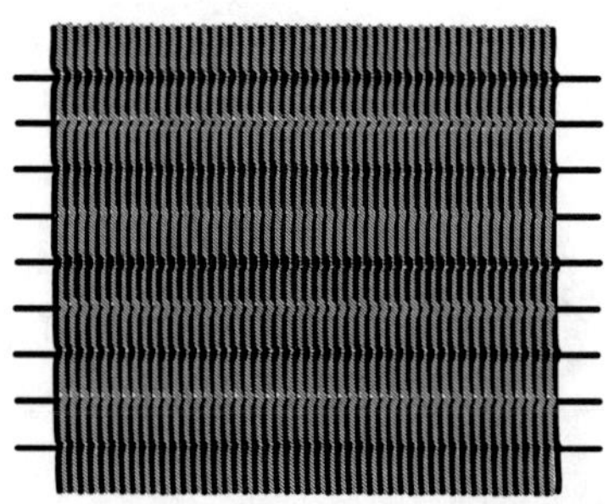

Finders Keepers?

Native Americans have many buried treasures. For hundreds of years, special objects would sometimes be buried with Native Americans, or maybe they would just be lost. Archeologists used to dig for interesting artifacts in old Native American gravesites. They would keep the Native American bones or the arrowheads, rattles, masks and other objects that they found. But this made the Native Americans feel like they were being robbed.

In 1990, the U.S. government passed a law that said that no one could look for or take these Native American objects anymore. And whoever had any already had to give them back to the people they belonged to. This is called repatriation

Help the archeologist return the artifact to a Native American.

Fast Fact

An artifact is an object that was made by people a long time ago for some useful purpose.

Busy Hands!

Before modern times, Native Americans didn't have stores where they went to buy things. They made everything they needed.

What did Indians make with their own hands? Use the Word Bank and pictures to find out!

Word Bank

blanket	moccasins	arrows	pottery	canoe
mat	food	jewelry	pouch	box

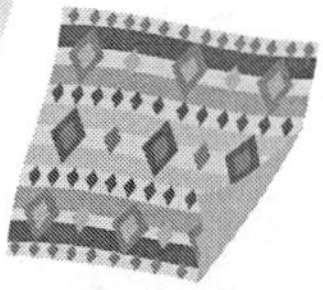 ___ ___ ___

 ___ ___ ___ ___

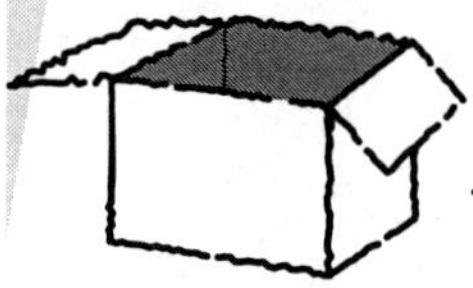 ___ ___ ___

 ___ ___ ___ ___ ___

 ___ ___ ___ ___ ___ ___ ___

 ___ ___ ___ ___ ___

 ___ ___ ___ ___ ___ ___ ___ ___ ___ ___

 ___ ___ ___ ___ ___ ___

 ___ ___ ___ ___ ___ ___ ___

 ___ ___ ___ ___ ___ ___ ___

American Indians Today

Beginning with the first letter of each group of letters, cross out every other letter to discover some new words. You may not have heard of these before, but you can read all about them!

1. Many Indians live on these, but many more do not!

TRYELSDEBRNVJAOTPIPOWNASX

____

2. Many Indians have been poor for a long time because for many years the government took away their lands and their ability to make a living.

TPKOOVWEBRNTXYA

____

3. Many Indians have been studying hard at school and going to college in order to earn more money. Education helps the Indians make their lives better. These Native Americans are working to become:

TSJUMCBCFEYSMSOFPUVL

____

4. This is a big term that means Native Americans have worked hard to get the U.S. government to let them rule themselves. This means that they have their own laws and make their own decisions. They are like a separate country inside the U.S.! Now, try and see if you can get your parents to give you the same thing!

TSGENLBF ***JDGEETSEWRAMCIHNUAKTYIKOTNU***

______________ ______________________________

Fast Fact

What do Indians work as today?

- doctors
- nurses
- factory workers
- artists
- lawyers
- actors

The same kinds of jobs any American might work at!

Native Americans Move to the City!

Solve the code to discover the mystery words!

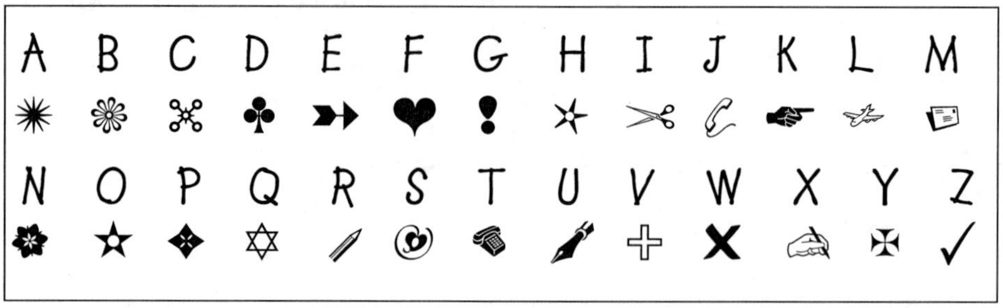

1. During the 1950s and 1960s, the American government paid Indians to leave their homes on reservations and move to cities to get jobs. If cities are sometimes called urban areas, then these brave Indians were called:

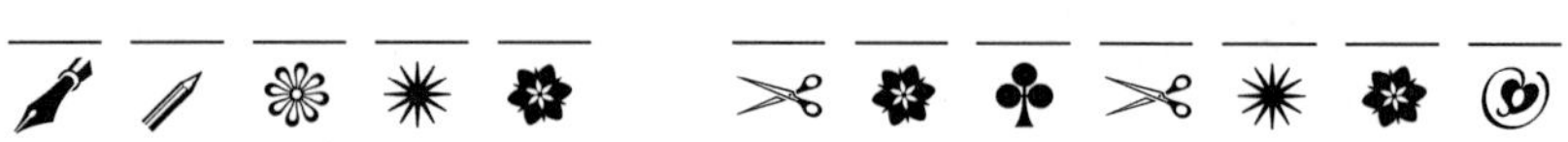

2. Many Indians chose to stay on their reservations and not move to the city. They thought that if they moved to the city, they would lose the way of life that their parents and ancestors had taught. These Indians called themselves:

3. Native Americans who moved to cities lived close to each other. They tried to keep their way of life as much as possible. They did not want to forget their religion, native art, or music. They did not want to lose their:

4. Are you afraid of heights? Many people are. The Mohawk Indians are not! Many of them work hundreds of feet above the city to build steel frames for skyscrapers. People who do this work above the city are:

5. Today urban Indians and reservation Indians come together to celebrate their culture. They share ideas and stories. They dance and beat drums. They make and sell Indian jewelry. During these celebrations, Indians remember how much they have to be proud of! These big parties are called